JUST ROLL WITH IT

JUST ROLL WITH IT

WRITTEN BY LEE DURFEY-LAVOIE
ILLUSTRATED BY VERONICA AGARWAL

RH
GRAPHIC

NEW YORK

Just Roll with It was thumbnailed with a 1.5 Faber-Castell pen and then penciled, inked, and colored digitally using a Cintiq 13HD and Adobe Photoshop CS5.1.

Text copyright © 2021 by Lee Durfey-Lavoie
Cover art and interior illustrations copyright © 2021 by Veronica Agarwal

All rights reserved. Published in the United States by RH Graphic, an imprint of Random House Children's Books, a division of Penguin Random House LLC, New York.

RH Graphic with the book design is a trademark of Penguin Random House LLC.

Visit us on the web! RHKidsGraphic.com • @RHKidsGraphic

Educators and librarians, for a variety of teaching tools, visit us at RHTeachersLibrarians.com

Library of Congress Cataloging-in-Publication Data is available upon request.
ISBN 978-0-593-12541-0 (hardcover) — ISBN 978-1-9848-9700-8 (library binding)
ISBN 978-1-9848-9699-5 (paperback) — ISBN 978-1-9848-9701-5 (ebook)

Designed by Patrick Crotty

MANUFACTURED IN CHINA
10 9 8 7 6 5 4 3 2 1
First Edition

RH GRAPHIC

A comic on every bookshelf.

To our family and friends, and my therapist. It's with your support, patience, love, and guidance that I'm able to become a better version of myself every day.
—V.A.

To everybody who needs to know they're not alone.
—L.D.-L.

Kids! It's time for dinner!

Coming!

Well, Jamie is starting her first year of college and Maggie is starting sixth grade tomorrow . . .

So I just wanted to take a moment to say how proud I am of you both.

It seems like only yesterday I was holding you in my arms, tiny samosas wrapped in hospital blankets . . .

Daaaad.
Quit it.

Anyway. Good luck
to both of you! Your
mother and I are
so proud.

Thanks, Dad.
Cheers.

Cheers!!

peek...

An eighteen . . . that's
an almost perfect roll.
I'm going to be fine.

18

There's no reason
to worry.

exhale...

4

6th Grade Math

Mr. Popkins

click

What do you think? Those two are definitely going to get eaten by that snake you saw, no question.

It wasn't a regular snake!! It was totally a python. Those things can eat, like, five people in a row.

HAHA HA HA HA HA HA

What the heck are they talking about?

hee hee

Who cares?

That guy was so rude.

I bet he's an eighth grader and thinks he can do whatever he wants because he'll be going to high school next year.

Yeah, I bet. Too bad eighth graders are at the bottom of the high school food chain.

ha ha ha

That's true!! I guess he'll get his next year, huh?

What's your favorite Chosen book? Mine's the third because Andor is *finally* recognized as the true king and his queen-to-be finds a dragon that they keep as a pet!

Um, well ...

I love the second one because--

Attention, class!

The first book we're going to be reading together this year is *The Crucible*.

The Crucible is about justice, lies, honor, fear, and persecution. It's almost always topical, especially today.

The Crucible

Maggie!!

The one where Strong Might and Saruta train together!

But wasn't it a little weird that Strong Might couldn't lift the car in that episode?

Yeah, but I think he wanted to show Saruta *they* could lift the car themselves!

I guess that's true. Strong Might's coolest trait is how much he cares for his heroes in training.

I have weaknesses . . . just like you!

Plus, it was cool to see someone so strong struggle like a regular person.

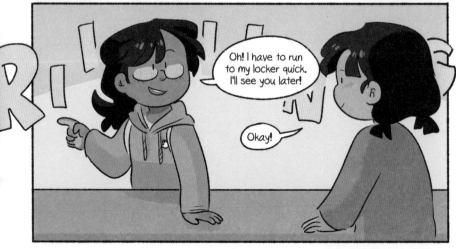

Oh! I have to run to my locker quick. I'll see you later!

Okay!

MR. ANR

6th GR

Welcome, students! Some of you may see science as an intimidating subject. But science doesn't have to be scary! It can be fun.

Students like you *and* Nobel Prize winners across the globe are working to solve the same puzzles.

Sometimes along the way, you discover puzzles you weren't even looking for! I'm excited to teach you the tricks to solving all the puzzles that you'll meet in life!

One puzzle is vast, but easy to see. The puzzle of the world around us!

The ebb and flow of the universe and the gifts and challenges that presents to us.

Does anybody know what a biome is? That's going to be one puzzle we endeavor to solve this year.

It's okay if you don't! We're going to find out together!

VRRR

beep

Oh . . . Clara's over there!

But it looks like she's busy with some other friends.

What if they're talking about me? What if they're *laughing* at me?

I'd just be bothering her.

I'll leave her alone.

24

zip

SLAM

Hey, kiddo!

How was school?

Hi, Eli. Hi, Alex. It was . . .

. . . okay, I guess?

26

Welcome home, Maggie. I've got snacks and chai in the kitchen!

It only costs one sentence about your day and the time it takes to wash your hands.

smek

Okay! Lemme just put my backpack upstairs first.

Pat

PAT

hOP!

Hi, Maggie!

Are we . . . I mean, are you excited for the day?

peek...

?

16

Yes! The book seems like it's gonna be sad, but Ms. Marian seems nice. I'm excited for Science too.

I'm really excited for Math. My mom showed me algebra over the summer and it seemed fun.

Excited? Fun? You're a strange one, Clara.

Hey, snake bait!

I wonder which one of you will get eaten first.

Shut up, dude!

They'll both get eaten at the **same time** because I hear it's like eight feet long!

BUMP

Do snakes have claws? I think I saw claw marks outside!

Today we'll be practicing the stitches that were on your worksheet yesterday. Take your time, and if you need more thread, let me know.

Needles . . .

Margaret?

39

Wait, hold on!! You have a cell phone, right?

My parents make me keep mine in my locker, but I can text you after school!

CLARA'S PHONE NUMBI

527—

Yeah!! I have one!! I'll add your number right away.

Okay, class!

44

SLAM

Click

How was school?

Did you make any friends?

Uh . . . yeah!

I made a friend and she likes the Chosen books AND *Super Justice High School*!

I want to text Clara now.

Shake shake

4

Only a four? She won't be annoyed if I text her!

SHAKE

Clara gave me *her* number *first.* I didn't even *ask!* So I should be rolling with advantage!

SHAKE

17

Thank you.

tap

It's already been one week! Everybody needs to tell me about their plans for the new school year!

I've heard some horror stories, but I think I lucked out this year. Only one kid cried so far and nobody's tried to pull anybody's hair yet.

It really makes me excited. This is definitely where I'm supposed to be.

You're going to be the best teacher that elementary school ever saw.

I'm thinking of officially starting a minor in mathematics as well as computer technology. It just feels . . . right.

Computers and numbers have always been your go-to, honey. I'm excited to see what you can do, even if I won't understand it.

Any goals for my favorite sixth grader?

Any clubs you want to join? Both of your sisters just "clicked" with their clubs, and I *know* you will, too!

Um . . . My goal is to get to seventh? School *just* started, so I don't really know . . .

Jamie and Eli are prodigies, but that doesn't mean *I* will be.

Well, I didn't mean it like that, sweetheart. I was just asking a question.

Can we talk for a second?

Yeah? What's up?

Ben and I have a chess competition to go to this weekend so . . .

So you have to leave CAT early?

Neither of us can make it on Sunday. I'm sorry.

That's okay . . . Good luck!

CLARA 8:27PM

P.S.!!! Surprise for
you tomorrow! Be there
or get drafted to work for
the evil king!!

We *have* to join!

I'd like to, but . . . I don't know if that's the right club for me, you know?

Why not?

My sisters were in academic clubs, and my mom was really impressed by that . . .

FIRST ANN...
ROBOTICS SHOW

1ST PLACE

Can I think about it?

10

So, what do we know about biomes so far?

Anybody?

Biomes are sections of the earth, but divided up into groups. The type of biome tells you what sort of things can live there, along with the temperature and stuff.

shFFF

Can I leave now?!

DASH!!

12

Oh my gosh!!

Gross!!!

HURRRK

Alex . . .

Cough

Cough

I'm sorry, Alex . . .

I'm fine . . . It's okay . . .

Maggie, what was that?! Didn't you hear me?! I *told* you Alex wasn't feeling good!

I *did* hear you, but . . .

Did you drop something? Do we need to go back?

No, it's just . . . My d20 said I couldn't move so . . . I didn't move.

What does that even *mean*?! Real life isn't CAT, Maggie!!

ZOOM

That was all your fault.

Now Eli is mad at you. You can't do anything right, can you?

That . . .

That's not true.

gasp

KNOCK
KNOCK
KNOCK

Hey, you. I'm sorry about earlier; I didn't mean to yell.

Knock knock

It's okay. I know you were just worried about Alex.

That's true, but I shouldn't have yelled. It wouldn't have mattered if you had gotten to the car faster.

Alex would've thrown up anyway. I'm sorry I hurt your feelings. Are you okay?

Yeah . . . I'm okay.

Okay. Listen, can I make it up to you? Everyone's around tonight. We could play a round of CAT, if you wanted.

No, thank you. Sunday is our special CAT day.

When we do CAT the next Sunday it won't be as fun. Then we'll do it any day of the week and Sunday won't be special anymore.

I want Sundays to be special still . . .

I think I understand. Mom's making an early dinner and she's almost done. Want to come down with me?

In a little bit. I didn't get any homework done yet.

All right. I'll see you later. If you need help just ask, okay?

Click

Dam it!

SHOVE

Margaret?

Tmp

Tmp

Tmp

SLAM

Am I going to be okay?

TAK TAK TAK

10

Ughh . . . that class was rough . . . My brain hurts.

Hey, snake bait!

High five!!!

ugh . . .

What? No hello? Are you afraid of me?!

Babies!!

blehhh

Leave us alone.

Jerk.

C'mon, Maggie, let's go.

SHOVE

1998

ACK!!

heh...

So, how does everyone feel about Sarah Good?

In the story, Sarah's community turns on her.

What do you think we can learn from this? How do you think Sarah must be feeling?

Jeez, Maggie, you're more tired than I thought. You really spaced out.

I'm gonna head to my locker before my next class. See you at lunch, okay?

Uh, sure! Yeah . . .

Maggie, are you sure you're okay? You seem really down.

Sigh

18

There's just, like, a lot going on. My sister thinks there's something wrong with me . . .

. . . and wants my mom to send me to therapy.

And my mom keeps asking me if I'm, like, amazing and perfect and cool like my sisters yet!!

But I'm *not* !!! I have no idea what club I want to join because I won't be as good as they were in their clubs and . . . !!

Maggie. Slow down!!

Sorry!! Sorry.

What do you want?

What do you mean?

Well . . . even if you don't have all the answers, can you pick something you want to do right now?

grrowwll...

To be honest . . . I wanna eat.

That's good!!

My grandpa says, "When it's hard to get through a tough time, you focus on the smaller things right in front of you."

If it's too hard to get through the week, then get through the day. If you can't get through the day, get through the hour.

Right now, you just have to finish lunch. That's all.

Do you know what club you want to join?

The RPG club for sure!

But just because I want to doesn't mean you have to! You should only join if it'll make you happy!

And if you try it out and you don't like it, that's okay, too!! You can always leave and join a new one if you want.

Huh . . . I didn't think of it that way. Thank you.

I'd like to try that. Making one decision at a time, instead of focusing on all of them at once.

Yeah!!

BRIIINGG

phew

wriggle

FLIP

They like you! It's because you pay attention in class.

Do you enjoy it?

Which I'll be collecting from you after you turn your book to page sixty-eight, section four of chapter three.

UUUUGHHH...

fwip

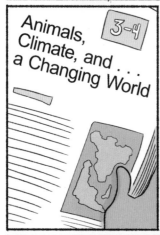

Animals, Climate, and . . . a Changing World

3-4

BRIINGG

READ CHAPTER 3
AND BE QUIET!!!

READ CHAPTER 3
AND BE QUIET!!!

KONK

Whuh?

SNAP

rustle rustle

Did you see that?

Something's out there!

You saw it, too, right?

Why are we standing up? Sit back down, everybody. You have reading to do.

There's something outside--

Sit down and read. If there's a problem outside, just ignore it.

That's one of the finer points of American history. You'll have to get good at it.

BR I I N G

But he has *superpowers!* We don't!

We don't even know what's out there!

hmmmm...

blurbl

Ugh...!

TMP TMP TMP

Maggie, are you all right? I brought you a flashlight.

SWING

Yeah, I'm okay . . .

Sorry, Mom, this is all my fault.

Your fault? Last time I checked you don't control the weather.

I don't but . . . I rolled a four. That's an awful roll. That's why the power went out.

On your die? What does that have to do with the power?

Uh . . .

BOOM

Never mind.

CRACK

100

Split down the middle . . .

Oh! I'll take that as plus two advantage.

Click

Thanks, house!

SHUT

That's true. I was really worried about making friends, too, but that turned out okay.

Just okay? Gee, thanks.

You know what I mean!

Did you see Mrs. Elefante with that bandage on her arm?

READ CHAPTER THEN ANSWER QUESTIONS 1—

She was digging in the bushes yesterday. I bet that thing bit her!

That's nothing! I saw the garbage tipped over and the meat from yesterday's lunch was thrown everywhere!!

I saw a torn gym shirt outside . . . I wonder if it's stealing from people's lockers because it likes the smell of humans!!

I bet it's so hungry, it's just dyin' for every little scrap it can get!

I can't do anything about that. All I need to focus on right now is my history reading.

One thing at a time. One thing at a time . . .

inhale

exhale

Just about everybody in my History class was freaked out!

That's nuts! I heard--

LET'S SEE SOME HUSTLE LADIES!

I've got to go get a book from my locker. I'll see you tomorrow.

yawn...

You can go on amazing adventures, like the ones from the books or ones you make up yourself!

That die that I always carry is called a d20. You use the d20 to decide how successful you'll be when performing an action.

If you hit the monster,

if you save the princess,

or if you notice the princess is lying to you . . .

BONK

. . . revealing that the monster and the princess were on the same side all along!

Is it ok if I stay late for the rpg club?

Of course kiddo! Pick you up at 5?

Yes please!

ok

here!

That was the *second* coolest thing that's ever happened to me!

The second?

?

Of course! The first was when you just saved my life!!

SHAKE SHAKE

Oh!

Here, you dropped this earlier, but I forgot to give it to you after all that stuff with the bully.

My journal!!

I didn't even notice it was gone . . . ! Thank you, Maggie, I'd be lost without this thing.

oof!

HONK HONK!

MAGGIE!!

That's my sister and her girlfriend. They're not usually so loud, I'm sorry.

That's okay!

I wish I had big sisters!

Do you want to come over for dinner?

Are you sure it's okay?

We'd be happy to have you!

Okay, thank you! I just have to text my mom.

tak tak

VVVRRRMMM

118

Hello, it's so nice to meet you! I'm Riya Sankhar, Margaret's mother.

Hello! I'm Clara. Thank you for having me over!

Of course, dear! Why don't you have a seat? Dinner will be ready soon.

Okay! Can I help you set the table?

So polite! Thank you! How are you liking school?

It's good!

Have you joined any after-school clubs?

Yes! Maggie and I joined the RPG club!

You did?? I always wanted to join! It seemed like so much fun!

Really??

I thought you liked student council so much!

Yes, I did, but RPG club is basically personal theater and creative writing all wrapped up in one.
I'm sure Maggie's going to have a lot of fun; it's run by Ms. Marian and she was Jamie's teacher.

She made me actually like reading!

Well, that sounds very exciting! I hope you two have fun!

Me too!

Yeah! Yes! I think . . . I think it will be good for me.

Me too! For me, I mean.

Now let's fight some monsters.

Okay. Thanks for checking, Clara.

Yo, hold on.

?

Hey . . .

Isn't that the kid who hit you with a textbook?

You bet I am!

Ugh, whatever. Shut up.

See ya, snake bait!!

Nice one!!

Part of the fun of science is the surprise of it... so here's a pop quiz!

4) What is the difference between how reptiles and amphibians lay eggs?

a) There isn't one.

b) Reptiles lay their eggs in water, and amphibians lay their eggs on land.

c) Reptiles lay their eggs on land, and amphibians lay eggs in water or damp media.

Skriiiitch

a) There

Reptile and amph and.

Should I use my die?

No! I know the answer! I just gotta think!

and land.

c) Re and a or dar

tick tick tick tick tick

Done!

Good job, Maggie!

Maggie, Clara! Over here!!

Come sit with us !

Have you actually had Ms. Marian for a class before?

She's an entertainer through and through! She literally uses "beguile" every week with us!

So what? Scholars can learn that spell, too! And Ms. Marian obviously got all her powers through studying!

They're arguing about which CAT class Ms. Marian would fit in best.

hee hee

MATH BINDER

GUMMIE SNAX

Sigh...

Doing okay?

Better than okay! I didn't know a day could go so good!

What happened?

I don't know why I was so worried about clubs. I made a lot of friends!

And they're all fans of CAT, too! Besides that, we're all pretty different.

Well, we saved a princess last time, but she was working with the dragon all along.

PARTNERS IN CRIME

Whoa, that sounds rough.

How about school? How's that going?

It's good! My Home Ec teacher says I'm getting better at sewing, and I'm learning about pollution and climate change in Science.

That's wonderful!

Did you know there might not be enough SPACE to plant TREES to suck up all the bad stuff in the air?!

That's terrible!

Did you know alligators can live in waters as cold as sixty degrees but can live in waters as hot as ninety degrees?

Or that chameleons change how their skin reflects light to change colors?

So you're learning a lot in school?

I want to be able to do stuff like that! I'd want to be pink!

BING BING

Do u have any CAT game books? NOBODY in group owns them irl

BWOOP))

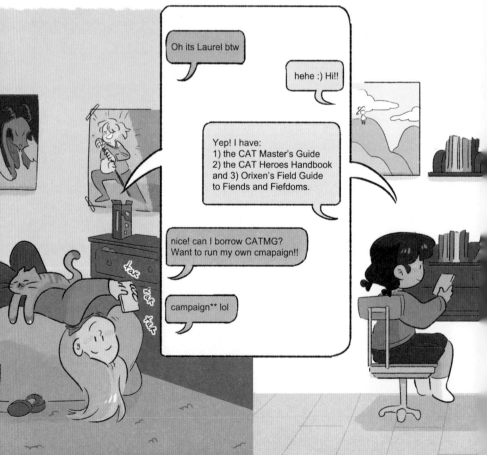

Oh its Laurel btw

hehe :) Hi!!

Yep! I have:
1) the CAT Master's Guide
2) the CAT Heroes Handbook
and 3) Orixen's Field Guide to Fiends and Fiefdoms.

nice! can I borrow CATMG? Want to run my own cmapaign!!

campaign** lol

i promise I'll take super good care of it!

you can check with our librarian

I have an awesome trakc record lol

FWUMP

I've never loaned it out before . . .

Hey, kiddo! Do you want to go to yoga with Alex and me? We could get slushies afterward.

Uh . . . you okay, Mags?

Is your book okay?

My friend wants to borrow it . . . but . . .

Clara? She seems like she'd take good care of it!

Fear or pain can't be avoided, no matter how much we try.

Coming out to Mom and Dad was really scary for me.

But I'm glad I did it. A lot of the worries I made up in my head ended up not coming true. So I put myself through a lot of heartache for nothing.

If your book gets ruined, that's necessary pain, because you're grieving something important to you.

But if you worry about touching it, then you never get to enjoy it.

You'd be putting yourself through unnecessary pain in the process of preventing pain. Does that make sense?

143

hug

Yeah. I think I get it. Thank you, Eli . . . You always know what to say. I wish I was smart like that.

Don't be smart like me, Maggie. That's no fun! Be smart like you!

You like science and art and writing. You can do things only you can do! You're only eleven!! Everything is going to turn out okay. It just takes time.

hee hee

I'm eleven and a half. My birthday is in a few months.

hee hee

144

145

I'm going to win! I'm going to get that sword!

You could try, but how will you succeed when I'm *always* with you? I can see your every move.

Every time you forget your homework,

or are afraid to ask a question,

and even when you're not sure if you want seconds at dinner?

That's me, reminding you that you're weak. You're shy. You're nothing.

wobble...

That's not true . . . ! I'm more than that!

shove

gasp

147

4:50

CAT CHAT
CLARA:

CAT CHAT
LAUREL: AAAAAAY DDD

SCROLL

YAWNN

Oh! Sorry.

It's okay, honey. We were actually just coming to talk to you.

Huh? What's going on?

Your mother and I have been talking, and we wanted to get your opinion on something.

150

SULK

Maggie?

Yeah?

Did someone steal your pudding that you were saving since last week? You look miserable.

No, I'm not upset about pudding. Are you speaking from experience?

Don't get me started.

I just want to take a nap and only wake up to play CAT. Is that too much to ask?

--saw something.

What are we going to do?

Huge teeth!

Did you see that thing again?

I don't know what we saw. But it didn't look friendly.

I can't believe the teachers say they haven't seen it. It was huge!

Rustle

Rustle

Good afternoon, class! Let's talk about survival!

What time? I have this, like, really important CAT game with my sisters . . .

That's okay! Whenever you want to come over is fine with me.

Oh, I just--

Okay, cool. What did you want to do?

KEEP RUNNING!!

POMU

NEWBIES!!

Please keep your voice down, Laurel.

What's going on?

YANK

We're all, like, stupidly beautiful and smart, but none of us can agree on what did this to Daniel's basketball...

So you two have to help us decide.

Something like a bug? Or maybe a really hungry rabbit?

The monster . . .

? ? Huh? A monster?

The *monster* that everyone's talking about! I've *seen* it!

Since you mentioned it to me I've heard almost everybody talking about something outside . . .

I've heard about it, too! It's supposed to be huge!

C'mon, why my basketball of all things?

I've heard about *something*, but I don't value anybody's opinion outside of this room. What did you see?

I didn't *see it* see it. I just saw something. A big red eye . . . and claws in the grass. Plus, I've seen the grass shake as it moves.

I've seen it from the windows and while walking outside too . . .

Well, there's only one thing to do in times of crisis like this!

LEAP!!

Phew . . .

Scuttle Scuttle

Earth to Maggie?

Uh . . . sorry.
I thought I saw
something is all.

My counselor said I might even finish school *early.*

!!

What if *I* left school?

What was that, dear?

What if I **left** school?

Honey.

Monsters aren't real. Are you playing too much of your catdog game?

Mom . . .

It's not just in my head! It's *real*!

SLAM!

I . . .

Slosh

gloop

I'm not crazy.

roll roll

THUNK

Can I text Clara?

Im worried.
I think there's a dragon.

A realnone
real one*

How do we fight a real dragon?????

TAK TAK TAK

After reading the assigned pages in *The Crucible*, complete the following short-answer questions. Remember to support your answers with examples from the book.

1. What are the personal limitations of one character, and how would you advise them to change?

Personal limitations?

Maggie! Dinner!

I barely started my English homework . . .

12

Just because they share a lot of screen time doesn't mean--

Calculations based on other shows we watch together--

Are you feeling okay now, dear?

Um, yeah . . . Sorry about before. Dinner smells great.

Are you okay?

I totally forgot to do the homework! I just got so, like, distracted last night.

Just one homework assignment isn't going to be the end of the world. I've missed stuff in History a few times and I still have a B+. Don't beat yourself up over it.

Sigh

Margaret!

Are you all right? It's dangerous to stop moving in the middle of the hallway. Get a move on.

Oh. Umm . . . Yeah, I'm fine.

Sorry.

Hey, Maggie! Are you okay? Did he yell at you?

I'm fine. He just told me to move.

Ms. Marian, our faithful dungeon master, is out because she has caught . . .

THE FLU!!!!!

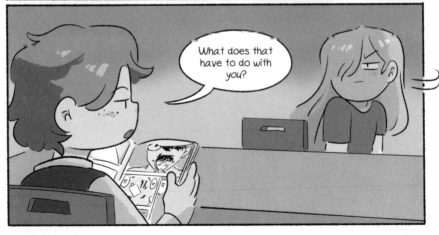

What does that have to do with you?

ANYWAY.

Because Maggie loaned me that book . . .

. . . I can run today's session successfully and amazingly.

Clap Clap clap

bow

Clap clap clap

ZIP

SLAM

Let's fight some zombies.

SLAM

FWOOM!!

SHOVE

Thank you for saving our village!

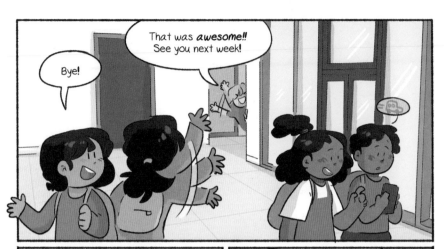

That was **awesome!!**
See you next week!

Bye!

I'm excited for Sunday! I can make really good shrimp; it's the only non-vegetarian thing I eat.

I didn't know you didn't eat meat!

There are many things you don't know about me, young hero.

wiggle wiggle

ha ha ha!!

One day of focusing on homework, and then we're gonna have the best Sunday ever!

HECK YEAH!

You two are going to be fine for Sunday, right? I'll *explode* if I have to miss another session!

Yes, Maggie, we'll be ready. I have a very good session in mind.

After the session I'm going to hang out at Clara's house. Sunday's going to be *amazing!*

Oh yeah? Look at you, Miss Popular!

I just have to get through Saturday.

beep HONK HONK

hel-- click

lo, click

hou--

se!

What's the rush?

Is there a fire?

I'm just excited for Sunday.

hop hop hop

? ? ? ?

Dear everyone, I got invited to a work party last minute, so I'm taking Mom out for a night on the town. There's money underneath the plate of hummus, so order some pizza! Save me a slice!
Love, Dad

Aww, that's good. They deserve it.

hahaha!

PiiZZAAA!!

Oh.

Peeel

+10 −10

tak
tak
tak

BROWNIE MIX

11

CRUNCH

I *think* she's asking if anybody's doing anything *fun* tomorrow.

Ha ha ha.

I don't think chess is boring! You're a brave strategist, and people's lives depend on you to stop the enemy!

You make us sound *awesome*, Mags. Thank you.

Your passion is so cool, Maggie. It's righteous.

Do you want to know what Eli and I are up to tomorrow?

We're going to the city because I've got a job interview! If I get hired, I'll be making prosthetics cheaper and cooler for kids.

OH MY REALLY?

ehehe

Congratulations, Alex. You've worked so hard for this!

Alex . . .

Would you guys have to move?

This part always gets me.

Huh? It's only 9:30?!

Why do I have to wait so long for tomorrow to come?

Oh. Because I'm supposed to?

Because I'm... not supposed to. Not supposed to what? Enjoy Sunday?

roll

Hi, Mom. Hi, Dad.

How was your party?

You should have seen your father try to dance! He's got two left feet.

Maybe, but I *did* impress the most beautiful person there!

Anyway... how are you, Maggie?

I'm okay. Just waiting for tomorrow.

Do you remember a few weeks ago, when your mother and I brought up therapy?

Yeah...? But I already told you, I'm fine!

We know, dear, but listen to our side of this. We're your parents, remember? We've been through a lot, and we can see when one of our children is in a tough spot.

But you're not *listening* to me! I'm okay! I'm okay! I'm passing my classes, and I'm in a club that I'm good at, and I have friends! What am I doing that's wrong?!

You're not doing anything wrong, Maggie. But when you flick the lights off and on . . . Or when you roll your little ball when we ask if you want more rice. That's . . .

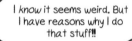

Weird.

That's not what we mean, sweetheart. It's just . . .

I *know* it seems weird. But I have reasons why I do that stuff!!

If I don't say hi to the house, then nobody else will.

It'll get lonely, and then it'll get sad! Then all the lights will stop working . . .

. . . or all the pipes will burst, or it will catch on fire!

These things aren't hurting you *now*, but what if you can't do them anymore?

What if you decide that's not enough, and you need to do fifteen different things before you can leave the house?

I don't know what you're talking about. That's not going to happen to me.

Just consider it, okay, Maggie? We just want you to be the best and safest you that you can be.

CLACK

Okay, gang. You're in high spirits after saving the town of Wyndale last week. You've since moved on, traveling down what *seems* like a peaceful forest road.

But you can tell...

...there's *danger* afoot.

217

FWING

AUGH!!!

THNK

THNK

Benji! Are you okay?!

dash

Yeah.

They won't get away with this!

CAW!

fwoosh

RAAAA

With the final knot tied around the bandits, you hand them over to the local townsguard.

The townspeople are elated that you've saved them twice now!

push

They don't have much, but they give you access to the oldest book in their library, which--

Maggie?

scoot

I have to get ready for my friend to pick me up. Thank you for the session. It was really fun.

?

tmp tmp tmp

h u g!

It's nice to see you again, Clara. Thank you for having Maggie over today. Here, share this with your parents.

Oh, thank you!

Thanks, Mom! Bye!

Hey, Maggie . . . can I show you something?

Of course.

I haven't shown anyone, not even my parents. It's just . . . I think I wanna do this, like, as a job.

But maybe I'm not good enough?

There are a lot of people who do it WAY better,

so maybe there's no point and--

Clara!!

Have you seen what I do when I don't feel confident?

229

You have magic, superheroes, a mystery, and all of it, like, *fits*! It's perfect!!!

You could be an artist!

You could make a TV show!

Or a movie!

Or a whole book series!

You have no idea how badly I've wanted to show you!

I'm sorry if I make things about me too much.

You don't! I I like being able to help you out . . .

. . . and I would let you know if it was bothering me.

Okay. Promise?

Promise.

You're a great friend. Also I want your autograph for when you get famous.

Oh, stop! You're embarrassing me!

How do you figure that sort of stuff out?

Oh, it's easy. You just pinch the end and--

No, not that.

How did you figure out what you wanted to do?

My sisters know what they want. And so do their partners. One of them is even getting a new job in the city!

And I... can't decide.

I need the d20 to tell me what I'm going to get for lunch.

I didn't know it was that bad...

Shrug...

Well, for me it was just something I liked to do. Every time we talked about TV or CAT... I thought of what I would do differently if *I* was making it.

I wasn't worried or second-guessing myself while I did it... It was just so much fun!

Do you have anything like that?

Maybe?

How do I know if I do?

I think sometimes you just... *know*.

POP

Huh. Maybe you're right.

KLATTER

WHOA!

Oh, goodness, Maggie, I'm sorry. Are you all right?

Oh! Uh--

Yeah, I'm fine.

klak
klak

GUMBALL SEARCH

Q OCD

SEARCH   HELP

What is OCD behavior?

What are the signs of OCD in adults?

Is OCD a mental illness?

TAP

NIMH » Obsessive-Compulsive Disorder
https://www.nimh.nih.gov> health> topics > obsessive compulsive...

WHAT IS OCD?

Obsessive Compulsive Disorder (OCD):Symptoms...

OCD is a treatable, though chronic, disorder
characterized by involuntary intrusive . . .

thoughts,

feelings,

images, or urges . . .

. . . called obsessions.

These are only relieved upon
acting out certain rituals . . .

Click
Click
Click

Am I gonna
be okay?

e x h a l e

. . . called compulsions.

OCD can also manifest as
obsessive thoughts, and
some people with the disorder
are unable to stop thinking,
worrying, or fixating on
certain subjects.

Compulsions may help these
obsessive thoughts go away,
but this is not always
the case.

People with OCD may find the anxious thoughts and rituals caused by the disorder disruptive to their everyday lives or routines.

And in very severe cases, this behavior can bring their lives to a standstill entirely.

There are many treatments to help manage the symptoms of OCD.

Therapy, cognitive behavioral therapy, and medication have all been found to be helpful.

If you believe you may have OCD, you should seek out the professional opinion of a therapist or your physician.

What's going on?

Recon is futile. I have no idea.

Somebody left their bike here over the weekend! The tires *and* frame got chewed through!

gasp!

Like . . . by a monster.

skrrt

tap
tap

I was right! I knew it! Something *is* out there!

What are we gonna do?

Paying attention in class is a good place to start, ladies.

Challenge of the Week!
problems

13. Solve the inequality and graph the solution on a number line

$$\frac{1}{3}y + \frac{1}{3}y$$

eometry

Without using a protractor find the measu angle B.

but using a protractor, find the measure

Everybody think of a plan and we'll talk after school!

Be safe!

You too.

SUBSTITUTE TE
MR. JONES
READ CHAPTE
BE QUIET!

Empty...

What happened to Mr. Anry?!

And his fish?

SNRK

Wuzzat?

Clara . . .

I think I'm a bad person.

What? Why?!

I didn't do my homework, and now Mr. Anry is gone! It's my fault!

No, it isn't!

Yes, it is! If I *had* done my homework, he would have had to be here to collect it, but I *didn't*, so the universe let the monster take him! Something bad happened to him because I didn't do what I was supposed to do!

Maggie, you're awesome, but the universe doesn't *care* if you do your homework or not. Whatever happened to Mr. Anry has nothing to do with you!

Okay? Breathe.

. . . Okay.

scoot

I know everybody is nervous. But the stories we tell together in this room can help. You can take on the things that scare you in a safe place here. That's what we've always tried to do, along with having fun.

Everybody ready?

I'm here to help, I promise. I won't hurt you!

How do I know you're not lying?

Because I'm terrified of you! You're in my nightmares, and you could kill me in an instant if you wanted to!

Very well.

Yeah. Well. Beth's bike got eaten up over the weekend. And Mr. Anry was absent, so people think something happened to him . . .

Do you want to stay home from school? I can talk to Mom for you.

No, it's okay. I need to go. I promised my friends I'd help them.

That's really brave of you, Maggie. Don't worry, you're gonna be fine.

What's going on? Why isn't anyone going to class?

They told us to meet at the auditorium instead. I think they're making an announcement about yesterday.

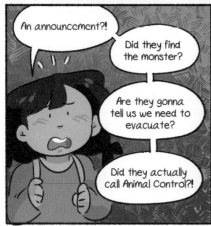

An announcement?!

Did they find the monster?

Are they gonna tell us we need to evacuate?

Did they actually call Animal Control?!

I don't know about any of that...

...but I DO know that I'm missing a history test. So for right now, that monster is doing me a solid.

What are we going to do if the school doesn't get rid of it??

That's easy!! We can just . . .

Hm.

I, uh . . . have no idea, actually.

Attention, students! Settle down!

I'd like to assure all faculty and tax-paying parents that our school is safe.

Z Z Z

There are no monsters, snakes, cryptids, or wild animals *anywhere* near here.

We're putting our most experienced custodian, Mr. Jones, on guard duty and he'll keep a watchful eye out for students' safety.

s~NRKK

PFFT!

We've also organized a field trip to a local wildlife refuge to assure you that nothing in the area can harm you.

Z Z Z

YEAH!

WOO!

Woo, field trip!

This is *good*, right?

I guess . . . I just can't stop feeling anxious. It's really annoying.

I know there isn't anything to be scared of, but I feel sick and I can't explain why.

I think the field trip will help. Going to the zoo with everyone will be a blast!

Yeah! I think you're right.

Maggie, Clara! Over here!

Is there an animal you want to see the most? I've never been to a zoo before.

17

I want to see if they have any tigers or big cats. I wonder if they would play with cat toys like normal cats do.

OMG

268

Red pandas!

Sooo cute!!!

It says . . . "red pandas were given the name 'pandas' before regular pandas"!

Oh . . . it says here they're on the endangered species list.

Get To Know...

The Red Panda!

Hey, guys! There are flamingos over there!

Wow, flamingos are pink because of the food they eat! And some can grow to be *five feet tall*!!

Whoa, they're--

Scary! They look like real-life *dragons*! They could totally eat a middle schooler.

They look like scaly dogs! They're just bathing in the sun, see?

People have killed *thousands* of them, but they've only hurt a few people. And they're on the endangered species list, too.

I think they're kinda cute. Especially the little ones.

SPOOK

CREW!

They're more likely to get spotted by hunters and prey, so they're more likely to get hurt or starve.

Plus, their lack of pigmentation effects their eyes and can make it harder for them to see!

We were able to help him, so he's not so scared of humans anymore.

We can't erase what happened to him, but look at him now!

Now his biggest complaint is that he doesn't get twenty meals a day like he so *clearly* deserves.

roll

Anyway, let's get you kids back where you're supposed to be. Your bus is leaving soon.

Wave wave

I'm really glad you were able to help Captain.

Me too!

Even though animals should be able to survive in the wild on their own, occasionally they need a little bit of extra help. That's what the rehabilitation center is all about.

People are the same way! Sometimes help is right in front of you. All you have to do is take it.

I can't count how many times Captain has been the one who helped me, even when I didn't realize I needed helping!

There's your teacher! You better get back!

Right . . . bye! Thank you!

grab

Clara... We have to save the school. The RPG club members are the only ones who know something is still out there.

We're the only ones who know anything about monsters!

I feel the same way. My little brothers are going to come here eventually. I can't let a monster eat them!

So how do we catch a monster?

Well, in CAT you can lure a dragon away with the promise of treasure, and a turtle-lion always gets distracted by pumpkin-boars. I think all we have to do is find the right bait.

?

Good thinking! I still have shrimp we can use. And we can bring fruit in case it doesn't like shellfish? I have frozen grapes.

Okay! What about a net to catch it in?

?
grapes
shrimp
middle schoolers

MONSTER FOOD PYRAMID

I think Daniel likes to catch butterflies . . . Maybe he has one?

I bet Laurel has his number.

Do you have Daniel's number? We need his butterfly net.

Clara and I are gonna catch this monster once and for all. And then we can all be like Captain and relax!

Yeah I have it.

But you have to let me help, cuz this sounds awesome. I'll text him right nowzzz

279

You look like you're feeling better. You were so nervous the other day.

Zz

I was, but not anymore!

I'm tired of always looking for monsters in the grass, looking behind me, second-guessing myself, or saying no to stuff I want to do!

Why were you saying no to stuff you --

B-because of the monster! But now we're gonna catch it . . .

So no one has to be scared anymore!

I can't wait until the day is over!

It better go by fast. I forgot an ice pack, and I have a lot of shrimp in my bag.

SNRK——!

ahaha!

Shh!!

Are you okay?

I'm actually . . . really nervous.

I know this is the right thing to do, but . . . what if I can't?

I'm not supposed to walk with you to class.

If I don't listen to the d20 now . . .

the bad luck will come back way worse later! Something horrible will happen!

But if you go the other way you'll be late!

Sorry.

It's okay.

R I L I N G G

The Crucible

I'll see you later. Be safe, okay?

I will! I have a lot of shrimp I can throw at something.

?

I believe you have the basics of sewing down, so now I want you to make something!

Start by sketching your idea out on paper. Once you're done, bring it to me and I'll help you turn it into a pattern you can sew!

You can make whatever you'd like, as long as it's appropriate for school.

Cool!

Anything, huh? I wonder what I should make?

roll

Oh!

Skrrtch Skrrt

Perfect!

a a a a—

?

Uhm, is everything . . .

. . . okay?

quiet...

I brought my nets, just like you asked. They're in my locker. But . . .

It's okay, Daniel! You don't have to come out with us. No one has to come along if they don't want to.

That's the thing. I *do* want to help!!

I want to be brave, like in CAT!

Me too! I don't know if I can hunt a monster . . . but I'm sure I can distract Mr. Jones so nobody gets in trouble!

We *all* wanna help, Maggie!

Thank you, everybody. We're going to find it. I know we are.

I'm going to avenge you, Mr. Anry. You *and* your fish.

Kids, settle down! No monster shenanigans in my gym class!

RAAAAAA

hahaha!

GUMBALL SEARCH

Q How to trap a wild animal safely

SEARCH HELP

NEWS SHOPPING :MORE

Sigh . . .

...pping Tips | wi.9.e1
= expert how. to. http
AP A WILD ANIMAL ui. wi.

How do you catch an animal with a live trap?

How do you trap a skunk?

Does animal control kill raccoons?

How do you set a catch-and-release trap?

Videos

Clatter

It's okay.
It's okay.
It's okay.

I'm okay.

inhale

I'm in control.

exhale

Everyone be sure to take some of this as well! We have grapes and shrimp as bait!

ew

Clara, this is the weirdest combo of snacks ever.

Are we ready?

Okay! Let's go catch a monster!

Is it ugly?

Are you *dead*?!

Is it huge?

N-no, it's . . .

A baby alligator.

Hello! This is Zoe of the Wildlife Rehabilitation Center. How can I help you today?

My friends and I captured a baby albino alligator at our school! Will you guys take care of him? I don't want him to get hurt!

Oh my gosh! Yes, we can take care of him, but our specialist is already on a call. Is there an adult around who can help you?

The local pound can come pick him up. Can I get your name and--

We have an adult! We can bring him!

Call my sister and tell her to come quick!

toss

nom

R-right, got it!

299

You caught a **WHAT?!**

Hi, Maggie's friends!

I can't take *all* of you with me! You'll never fit in our car!!

hey, sis...

You don't have to! Just luke Maggie and Clara!

The place closes at six and it's already 3:40! It took us *ages* to get there the other day!

Did you go by bus?

Yeah.

300

They went the long way to avoid the tolls! We can get there faster if we take the highway!

ZOO

But I'm eleven! I don't have any money!

Crap, I didn't bring my wallet.

It's okay! I always keep an emergency twenty in the glove compartment. Let's go!

WOW, YOU ARE SO SMART!! AND RESPONSIBLE!!

heh

Thanks for all your help, guys!! We'll be back!!

Believe it or not, I rolled a one.

You did all that even without your die telling you it would go well? Weren't you nervous?

I was!! And I still am!! But I knew we had to do it, and I'm glad we did. Doing something even though I was scared felt . . . kind of amazing.

You're amazing.

exhale...

...breathe in...

...and out.

Here to slay me, child?

What is the use? Look how I've grown. You'll never best me now.

I'm not here to slay you. I'm here to help you.

What?! You help me? A near-perfect being? I have to laugh!

Because you're a part of me. I want us to become the safest and best version of Maggie that we can.

POOF

AUGH?!

You seem tired this morning.

Yeah I--

Mr. Anry!!

You're back! We thought you got eaten!!

Not that I know of!

Why were you absent?

Well . . . I'm going on paternity leave! My daughter was a bit eager to say hello and scared my wife and me, but everything is okay now.

I'll bring pictures of her to class if you fill me in on this alligator fiasco I've been hearing about.

Deal!

Yes, I think that's true.

Really?

Yes. Eli told us that when someone has anxiety, it's like they have an extra load on their brain all the time.

Some fear is necessary. Fear teaches you not to put your hand on a hot stove. But when anxiety overwhelms us . . .

. . . you may not be able to use a stove at all. And *that* interferes with day-to-day life.

That's why we wanted you to see a therapist. They can give you tools to control your fear, so it doesn't control you.

That sounds really nice. I want to be able to do that.

I'm so proud of you, Maggie!

Me too!

I can't believe you caught the monster terrorizing Lilac Valley Middle School!

Aw...

He's not so scary once you get to know him.

Smoosh

So, who's ready for next week?

Midterms are over! Which means on Monday I get to run a brand-new campaign . . . all by myself!

clap clap CLAP CLAP

tweet

Thank you, thank you.

Come on, guys! Maggie's dad said we could meet him by the food court for lunch, and I'm starrrrving!

Speaking of CAT . . .

I made you this in Home Ec. For being my best friend! And for helping me join RPG club.

Wow . . . I love it! Thank you!

SQUEEEEE

This is gonna bring me sooo much luck in Laurel's next game! Twenties all day, baby!

Can you come over after RPG club on Monday? My moms want our help with dinner again.

I'd love to, but I can't. I have my second therapy appointment.

ALzigorth

CHARM	PWR	HP
4	7	10

ExP

Inventory

NOTES

Likes
- Peace
- marigolds
- Her Axe
- Carliene

Dislikes
- fighting
- Evil King Leo
- Snakes
-

"I'm fighting for a world where no one has to be afraid!!"

Carliene

CHARM **8** PWR **4** HP **10**

ExP

Inventory

NOTES

Likes
• Alzigorth
• Magic
• Gold
• Animals

Spells
• Ward
• Grace Period
• Control
• Pause

"We are fighting for a world where no one has to be afraid."

A graphic novel page from Start to Finish!!

Step 1 - Script

The script for this book was written by my partner, Lee! He wrote almost all of *Just Roll with It* using Google Docs on his phone.

we have a computer

tAK tAK tAK

Page 58:

1) The bell rings and Maggie is watching the grass this time as she walks to her sisters car.

2) The grass is moving and above and around it we see the whispers of some of the things she's overheard so far: 'six feet long', 'red eyes', a 'snake' 'six legs' etc.

Maggie is frozen where she stands, eyes wide.

3) The grass shakes again and she takes a step back, pulling out her d20.

4) She looks down at the d20 and it shows a four.
Maggie (outloud): What can I do? Can I run?

Step 2 - Thumbnails

After Lee is done with the script, I print it out and put all the pages in a huge binder. I draw thumbnails directly on the script pages using a 1.5 Faber-Castell marker!

fwUMP

It's my favorite for thumbnailing because it helps me stay loose.

Like, *really* loose.

Step 2.5 - Get References

Step 3 - Pencils

The majority of the heavy lifting is done during this stage, but penciling is a lot of fun even so!

I do a lot of problem solving here, but thankfully things are pretty forgiving.

I love using Photoshop and working digitally because I'm able to resize pieces if they don't fit right, move them around, etc.

Tools

Cintiq 13 HD

MacBook Pro

Photoshop CS 5.1

Step 4 - Inks

At this point I've already decided line widths for everything, so inking is pretty mindless in the best way. I like to put on Let's Plays, anime, cartoons, or music and just chill when I ink.

For the most part, it's pretty smooth sailing. Though I do run into the occasional *blob-of-unknown-intent*, and I have to puzzle out what pencil-me was thinking when she drew it.

Step 5 - Color

Almost done! I flat the entire page before going in for coloring. Flatting is the first pass to make coloring easier. My best friends in the whole world, Alex and Wren, were a huge help with this!

Another big change that I made during this stage was adjusting the third panel. It was really bland up until the coloring stage, so I decided to rework it. It took a bit of playing around until I settled on something I liked.

Which do you like better, Cappy?

shrug

Step 6 - Preparing for Print

The last step is focused on prepping the book for print. This includes resizing the pages, making sure they're formatted for CMYK printing and any other requirements! The requirements can differ from publisher to publisher.

This whole process took us a year or so, and now you have the final book in your hands. Wow!!!!

Thank you so much for picking up *Just Roll with It*. I hope you enjoyed it!

THE END

Authors' Notes

In 2017, I brought up the possibility of me having OCD with my therapist of several years. After we started discussing it, a lot of things began to make sense. Previous depictions I had seen or things I had read about obsessive compulsive disorder involved physical tics, repetitive actions, counting, or cleaning. But as I learned more about the disorder and how it presents, I realized that things in my everyday life—things I had grown accustomed to and deliberately worked around—could all be traced back to obsessive thinking and compulsions: my tendency to be very picky about food, my meticulous overplanning in order to avoid being uncomfortable in any situation, my fear of dying and death . . . and my rituals to keep it at bay.

Once I gave it a name, I started to identify the different ways it had a hold on me. I wanted Maggie's story to highlight how OCD can take you hostage. Over the course of developing this story, I was worried Lee and I weren't showing enough types of symptoms. But, in truth, there was no way we were going to be able to represent every possible OCD manifestation and condense it into one story. My hope is that Maggie can help someone else's light bulb go off and give them the first push they need to look deeper if their anxiety is limiting their quality of life.

The advice that Maggie's therapist gives her at the end is taken directly from my own therapist, Debbie. I want to reiterate that what's most important is your own journey to mental well-being and not necessarily "fitting" a diagnosis perfectly. I also want to take the time in this author's note to encourage you to shop around for therapists, if you're interested in seeing one. It may take a bit of time until you find someone who is a good fit for you.

Thank you for reading *Just Roll with It* and this author's note. I hope that reading this story has given you as much as it has given me to create it.

 Veronica Agarwal

For me this book was inspired by being miserable in middle school. I went undiagnosed with depression, anxiety, and ADHD for a really long time, and it made certain parts of growing up incredibly difficult. My deepest hope is that this book, and Maggie's story, can help someone feel even just a little bit better about going through that sea of seemingly unending awkwardness and fear.

 Lee Durfey-Lavoie

About the Authors

Veronica Agarwal (she/her) is a cartoonist and an illustrator from New York. She lives with her partner, Lee, and their three cats. She graduated from the School of Visual Arts with a BFA in cartooning. She's been featured in *Elements: Fire, Power & Magic: The Queer Witch Comics Anthology, Electrum,* and *When the Rules Aren't Right* by Leslie Tolf. She also illustrated *Alexis vs. Summer Vacation,* written by Sarah Jamila Stevenson. Her work aims to normalize talking about mental health through stories that are enjoyable and uplifting. She loves sunflowers, summertime, and dogs! wisbafolio.com 🐦 @anuanew

Lee Durfey-Lavoie (he/they) grew up in Rhode Island but now lives in New York. Along for the journey are his three cats (Captain, Natasha, and Sammy), who both drive him up the wall and keep him sane. A proud college dropout, this is his debut graphic novel. He likes folk music, cats, and coffee. 🐦 @DurfeyLee

Acknowledgments

I acknowledge that this was written and drawn on land stolen from Native Americans, specifically from the Merrick tribe.

I want to thank my entire family—Mom, Dad, Lee, Grandma Dadi, Grandma Nana, Aunt Fran, Aunt Theri, Aunt Tracy, Uncle Andy, Uncle Ted, Matt, Steve, Mary, and Amanda—for being the best family I could possibly ask for. From when we're serious to when we're silly, being a part of this family is always a blessing. To Lee's family, for welcoming me with open arms and hearts and incredibly comforting hugs.

To Alex and Wren, for being my best friends and helping me flat this book during crunch time. To Anthony, for inspiring me to be passionate without remorse. To Paloma, for her laser-focused critique and for being a friendly ball of energy. To Alisa, for inspiring the title of this book, and to Krav, for their assistance on backgrounds. To everyone in Sunflower Station, it should probably be considered a hazard to have this much talent and kindness condensed into one Discord server. Starting Sunflower Station will always be my proudest achievement.

To my agent, Susan Graham, thank you for your hard work, knowledge, and kindness. This book exists in huge part because of you. I'm so proud of being your client. Thank you for having me!

To Gina Gagliano, who saw potential in Lee and me and gave us this opportunity. To Whitney, Patrick, and everyone at Random House Graphic, thank you for allowing us to stand among a lineup of such beautiful books.

To my cats, Natasha, Captain, and Sammy, thank you for keeping me company while I worked on this book. Sometimes you yelled, sometimes you demanded attention, and you walked all over my keyboard, but I wouldn't have had it any other way.

And finally to Lee, writer, partner, and love of my life. When I was a kid, there was a huge swath of media that told me that relationships were supposed to be work, but being with you has been the easiest thing I've ever done. I always assumed I would have to sacrifice parts of who I was if I wanted to find a long-term partner. You have never made me feel like you love me for anything less than what I truly am, and for that I thank you.

—V.A.

Acknowledgments

Firstly I'd like to acknowledge that this book was written on stolen Merrick land.

Secondly I'd like to say thank you to the team at Random House Graphic who was with us every step of the way, encouraging us and helping this book be the best it could be: Whitney Leopard, our wonderful editor, who has been inspiring and supportive since day one; Gina Gagliano, who took a chance on us and let us add to RHG's wonderful mission of getting a graphic novel on every shelf; Patrick Crotty; Nicole Valdez; and everybody else at Random House and Random House Graphic.

I'd like to thank, of course, Susan Graham, who is the best agent and friend one could ask for. They guided us and made this book possible, helped give it life and a solid foundation. They helped not just the book get off the ground but me as well, and I would not be where I am without their help. My deepest and never-ending thanks and gratitude.

To my family, who, if I named everyone, this would go on for way too long. But to my mom, especially, for being the kindest, gentlest, and most hardworking person I know and who taught me to be strong and kind and compassionate. To my siblings, who, while I don't talk to them often enough, inspire me daily and were the driving force behind this book. To my grandparents and dad for always being there when I needed them. To Veronica's whole side of the family, who accepted and loved me from the beginning, I literally wouldn't have survived without you. I love you all so much. To everybody else: thank you so much. I appreciate you more than words can say.

To my friends in Sunflower Station and beyond, for being the nicest, funniest, weirdest people in the world.

And finally to Veronica, my artist, co-author, and partner, and the love of my life. The well of love, support, and encouragement you offer me has transformed my entire life and made me a better person. I can't begin to describe how much you mean to me, but this book, this career, and everything else would never be possible without you by my side. I love you.

—L.D.-L.

FIND YOUR VOICE
WITH ONE OF THESE EXCITING GRAPHIC NOVELS

PRESENTED BY RH ◼ GRAPHIC

f ◎ @RHKIDSGRAPHIC

A GRAPHIC NOVEL ON EVERY BOOKSHELF